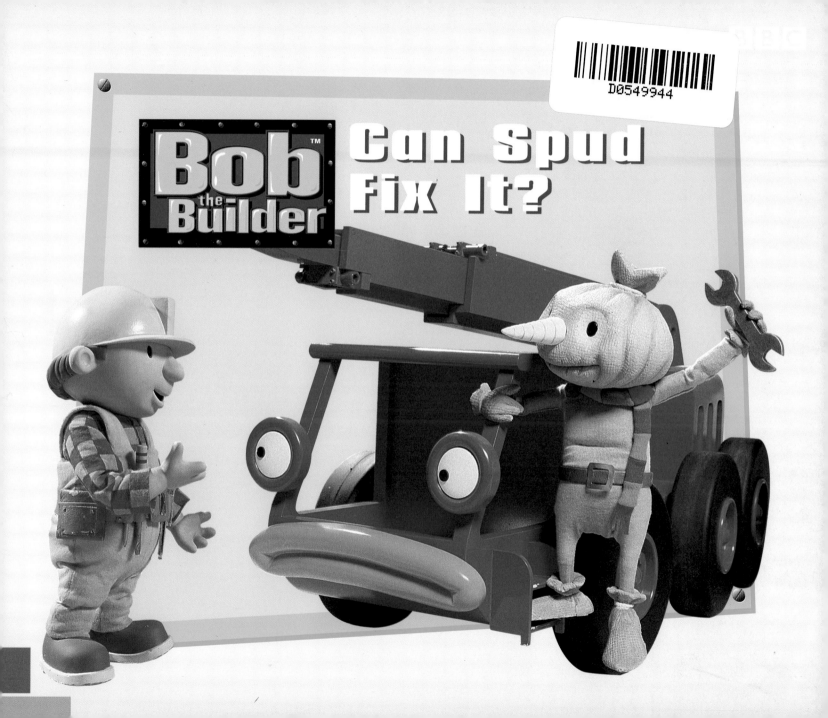

Bob the Builder™

Can Spud Fix It?

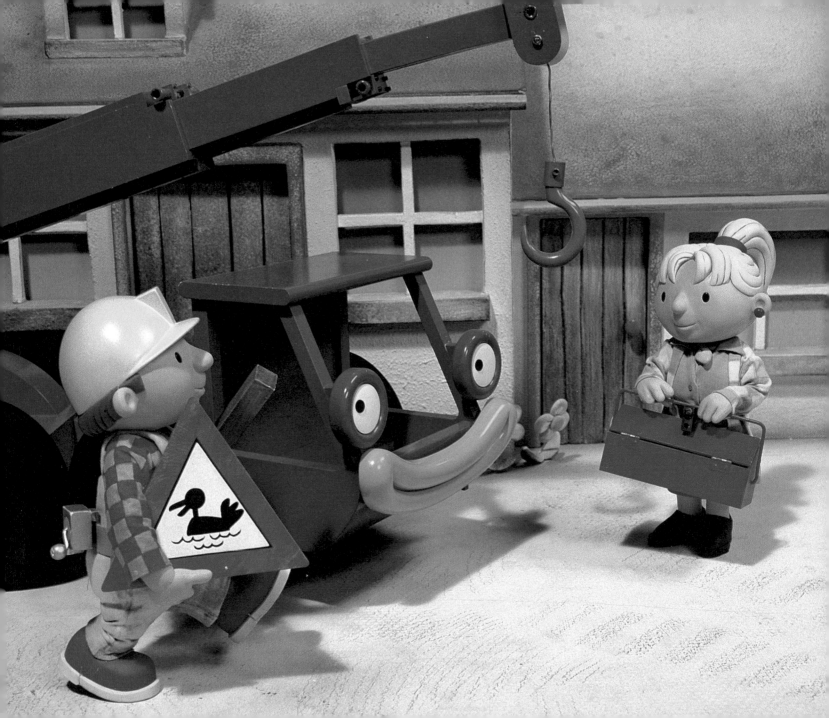

It was early morning in Bob's Building Yard. Bob was getting ready to go to the pond and put up a new sign.

"Here's your toolbox," whispered Wendy, as she passed him the heavy box. "Why are you whispering?" asked Dizzy.

"Roley and Muck worked late last night," Wendy replied. "So we're giving them a few hours extra sleep."

Bob climbed aboard Scoop. "Let's go," he said leading Lofty and Dizzy out of the yard.

Down the road Spud was complaining to Travis.

"Being a scarecrow isn't as easy as you think," he grumbled.

Suddenly the rickety old gate he was leaning against gave way and Spud fell flat on his back.

"Hee, hee, hee!" giggled Travis.

"Right, that's **it!**" said Spud crossly. "I'm going to get a new job. I could be a pilot!"

"You can't fly!" laughed Travis.

"I could learn," insisted Spud. Spreading his arms like aeroplane wings, he screeched up and down the road.

Bob and the machines came chugging around the corner and almost crashed into Spud.

"Look out!" yelled Bob. Scoop slammed on his brakes sending Bob's toolbox flying.

"Spud! You know you should never play near roads!" cried Bob.

"Sorry, Bob," muttered Spud.

"Could you go and tell Farmer Pickles that I won't be able to fix the window frames in the old cottage until tomorrow?" Bob asked the naughty scarecrow.

"I'm on the job, Bob!" grinned Spud.

As Bob and the team headed off, Spud found Bob's toolbox lying by the side of the road. "Forget Spud the Scarecrow!" he cried as he pulled out a bright shiny spanner. "From now on I'm **Spud the Spanner!** I'm going to be a builder, just like Bob!" "Really?" rumbled Travis, deeply impressed. "The first thing I'm going to fix is that broken gate!" chuckled Spud.

When Bob got to the duck pond he discovered that his toolbox was missing.

"My favourite new spanner's in it," he moaned.

Bob asked Lofty to go back and see if it had fallen out during the journey.

Lofty nervously did a three point turn and rumbled off to look for the missing toolkit.

Meanwhile Spud was mending the gate.

"It looks a bit wobbly," Travis remarked.

"It's meant to look like that!" Spud insisted.

"This building stuff's easy," he continued, "I think I'll go and fix the cottage windows next. You can be my machine, Travis," Spud suggested.

"Oh, no! Not me!" cried Travis.

"Farmer Pickles wants me to plough a field this afternoon." And with that Travis drove off.

Spud set off down the lane where he found Lofty looking for Bob's toolbox.

"Is this it?" asked Spud, holding up the toolbox he was carrying.

"Er, yes," Lofty said nervously. "C… can I have it, please?"

"Only if you help me with a bit of building first," Spud said.

Lofty didn't really like the idea but he agreed to help.

"**Hurray!**" yelled Spud as he jumped onto Lofty, "I've got a machine! Now I'm a proper builder. Lofty and Spud are on the job!"

At the duck pond Bob waited and waited for Lofty.

"I'd better phone Wendy and get her to send my spare box over," he told Dizzy.

Wendy sent Muck off with the spare toolkit straight away. On his way he bumped into Lofty and Spud.

"Can't stop, Muck," said Spud importantly, "We're busy."

As Spud and Lofty roared past, Muck noticed Bob's other toolbox dangling from Lofty's hook.

"Hey, **STOP!**" he yelled.

Spud and Lofty pulled up outside the old cottage.

"I think I'll start on the front door," beamed Spud.

"Erm… well… are you sure you know what you're doing?" dithered Lofty as he lowered the toolbox to the ground.

"Don't worry! Spud the Builder's on the job!"

"Oh, er…," whimpered Lofty, "I can't look!"

Bob, Scoop and Dizzy were feeding the ducks when Muck came panting up to them.

"Bob! Bob!" he spluttered as he tried to catch his breath. "I've just seen Lofty with Spud. Spud's got your lost toolbox and he's on his way to fix the old cottage!" Muck gasped.

"Let's go team!" cried Bob as he jumped aboard Scoop. "We've got to stop Spud before he hurts himself!"

At the old cottage, Spud stepped back to admire his work.

"Not a bad job!" he said proudly.

Lofty clanked nervously. "Er, but… erm… all the windows are crooked!"

"That's how they're supposed to look!" laughed Spud. "Come on, Lofty," he added excitedly, "We've got another job to do. One of the barns has a bit of the roof missing and we're going to fix it!"

Bob arrived with Scoop, Muck and Dizzy. They couldn't believe their eyes when they saw the mess Spud had made of the old cottage.

"Oh, no!" cried Bob. "We'd better sort the windows out before there is an accident. I wonder if there's anything else that needs fixing?" Bob said as he leant back on the door, which collapsed.

"**Ahhh!**" yelled Bob as he fell over backwards.

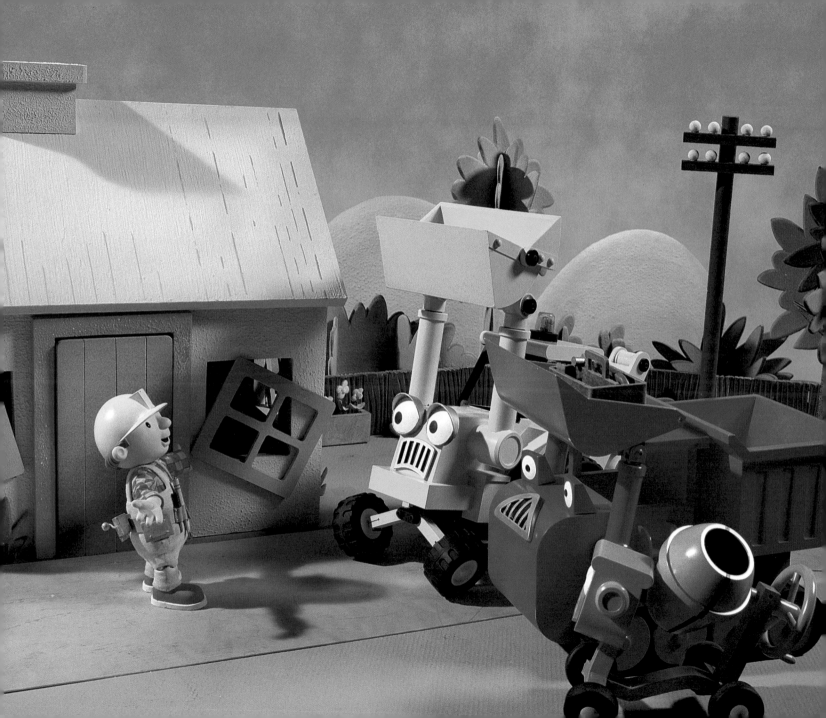

At the barn Spud strapped a sheet of roofing onto his back, and got Lofty to lift him onto the roof.

"This is exciting," he said, "I've never fixed a roof before."

"Be careful, Spud!" pleaded Lofty.

"Don't you worry," laughed Spud. "This is a job for Spud the Spanner!"

Just then a huge gust of wind blew him off the roof! Spud sailed through the air like a bird, high above Lofty's head.

"**H-E-L-P!**" cried Spud as the wind blew him on.

Back at the cottage, Muck looked up at the sky. "What's that?" he wondered.

"**Wow!**" Dizzy squeaked excitedly. "It looks like a flying Spud!"

They all stared up at Spud who was flying straight towards them.

"**Whey! Arrrghh!**" Spud bawled as he landed on the chimney of the old cottage.

"Nice landing, Spud," chuckled Bob.

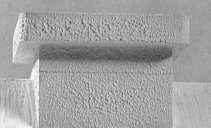

Bob said he would only get Spud down if he promised **never** to use his tools again.

"It's very dangerous," he told the naughty scarecrow. "You could have got hurt."

"Ummm, I'm sorry, Bob," mumbled Spud.

"And where's my toolbox?" asked Bob.

"Er, it's all right Bob," said Lofty as he came clanking up, "I've got it."

"Well done, Lofty," said Bob.

"**Now** you can bring Spud down."

Lofty gently lifted Spud off the roof.

"I think I'll stay a scarecrow," Spud announced. "It's *much* safer than being a builder!"

THE END!